Teachers — and parents of a large family know from experience that children learn to read in many different ways. Some learn quickly and easily, some learn slowly, some struggle heroically and some, it seems, will never learn.

Many schools and school systems in the United States are now using and experimenting with this alphabet. Perhaps it will be helpful to your child or to a child you know. In any case, why not try it? It's fun.

—Eileen Clark, Director
Head Start Program
Danbury Public School System

LOTHROP, LEE
& SHEPARD CO., INC.
NEW YORK

jœsi and the snœ

HELEN E. BUCKLEY

Illustrated by Evaline Ness

Second Printing, June, 1965

wun dæ
when it woz snœiŋ
jœsi wœk up nœiŋ
that sœn
ʃhɛɛ wʊd bɛɛ gœiŋ
out tʊ plæ.

ʃhɛɛ'd get her sled
and bundl up,
tæk dœzy cat and buttercup,
mæk a paþ tœ charlz-þe-mous
œver in hiz littl hous,
and aull þat luvly snœy dæ
þhæ wœd plæ
and plæ
and plæ.

but when ʃhɛɛ askt ʒhe dœzy cat

tѡ gœ out in ʒhe snœ,

ʒhe dœzy cat sed nœ.

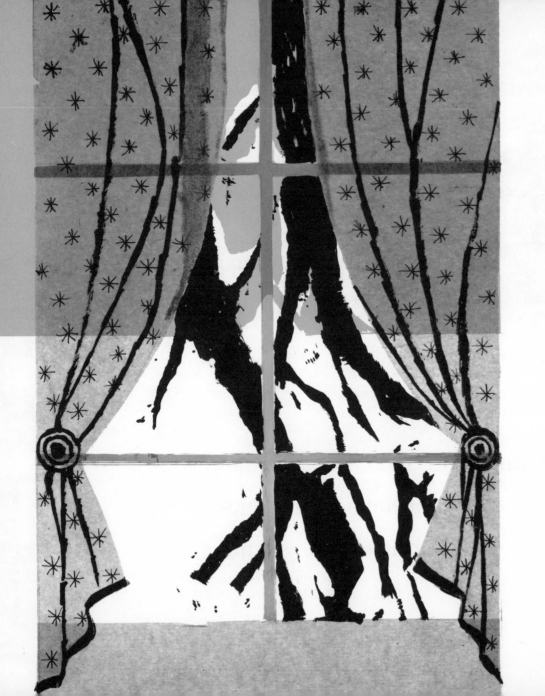

the snœ
woz much
tœ deep

and hee
wœd rather
sleep.

and when ʃhεε askt her littl dog
tω gœ out in ꝼhe snœ,
buttεrcup sed nœ.

hee'd rather
curl up
in his bed

than goe
slieding
on a sled.

and whot about charlz-the-mous
œver in his littl hous;
wœdn't hee
liek tω gœ
out in aull the snœ?

nœ.
charls wœd rather
dreem ov chees
than ried dœn hill
on slippery skees.

sœ jœsi askt her muther, her daddy and her bruther,

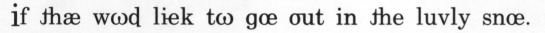

if thæ wod liek to goe out in the luvly snœ.

"græt scot!"

"whie not?"

"thær'ʒ lots ov snœ!"

"let's gœ!"

and sœ
ꝥæ aull
bundld up,
left
dœzy cat
and buttercup
sleepiŋ on
ꝥær cœzy beds,

tʊk ðær sausers, skees, and sleds,
and went out in aull the snoe—

aull the deep and luvly snœ.

ꝼhæ sliꝺ ꝺoun hillꝭ,

tʊk sum spillꝫ;

mæd a snœman,

fed the birds;

Saŋ sum soŋz with snœy wurdz,

mæd a path tω ᴄharlȝ-the-mⲟus

ⲟever in his littl hⲟus,

and had a luvly snœy dæ—
a luvly, blœy, snœy dæ.

and when
ᚦhæ cæm
insied at last,
sorry ᚦhat
ᚦhe dæ woz past,

ꝥhæ bilt a fier—
red and rœsy,
pʊt on slippeɹʑ—
waurm and cœzy,

then
everywun
just curld
riet up
with
dœzy cat
and
buttercup
and went tω sleep.